Around the Table That Grandad Built

Melanie Heuiser Hill   illustrated by Jaime Kim

CANDLEWICK PRESS

This is the table that Grandad built.

These are the sunflowers picked by my cousins
Set on the table that Grandad built.

These are the napkins sewn by Mom

Surrounding the sunflowers picked by my cousins
Set on the table that Grandad built.

These are our plates—red, orange, and yellow . . .

That go with the napkins sewn by Mom
Surrounding the sunflowers picked by my cousins
Set on the table that Grandad built.

These are the glasses
    from Mom and Dad's wedding . . .

Set by our plates—red, orange, and yellow—
That go with the napkins sewn by Mom
Surrounding the sunflowers picked by my cousins
Set on the table that Grandad built.

These are the forks and spoons and knives—
gifts from Dad's grandma long ago . . .

Placed by the glasses from Mom and Dad's wedding
Set by our plates — red, orange, and yellow —

That go with the napkins sewn by Mom
Surrounding the sunflowers picked by my cousins
Set on the table that Grandad built.

This is the squash that took over our garden.
These are the potatoes and peppers we roasted.
And these are the beans, overflowing the bowl!

This is the stack of toasty tamales.

These are the samosas, spicy and hot.

And this is the rice pudding we have every year.

This is the bread—still warm!—that Gran baked.
This is the butter made by us kids.
And this is Dad's huckleberry jam—
mmmMMMMMM.

And *here* are the pies! I made this one myself!

For these hands we hold,
for tasty good food,
for family and friends,

for grace that is given
and love that is shared,

we give thanks . . .

around this table that Grandad built.

For Mom and Dad, who bake and build
and gather us around the table
M. H. H.

For my family
J. K.

Text copyright © 2019 by Melanie Heuiser Hill
Illustrations copyright © 2019 by Jaime Kim

First edition 2019

Library of Congress Catalog Card Number pending
ISBN 978-0-7636-9784-6

19 20 21 22 23 24 CCP 10 9 8 7 6 5 4 3 2 1

Printed in Shenzhen, Guangdong, China

This book was typeset in Youbee Bold.
The illustrations were done with acrylic paint, crayons, and digital tools.

Candlewick Press
99 Dover Street
Somerville, Massachusetts 02144

visit us at www.candlewick.com